This edition first published in the United Kingdom in 2016 by
Pavilion Children's Books
1 Gower Street
London WC1E 6HD

An imprint of Pavilion Books Company Ltd.

Design and layout © Pavilion Children's Books
Text and illustrations © Rosie Wellesley

ISBN: 9781843653097

A CIP catalogue record for this book is available from the British Library.

10 9 8 7 6 5 4 3 2 1

Reproduction by Tag, UK
Printed by 1010 Printing, China

This book can be ordered directly from the publisher online at
www.pavilionbooks.com, or try your local bookshop.

To Izzie,

Happy 1st Birthday!
Love from
Isla x

I hope you enjoy this book as
much as I do! ☺

Wide-awake Hedgehog

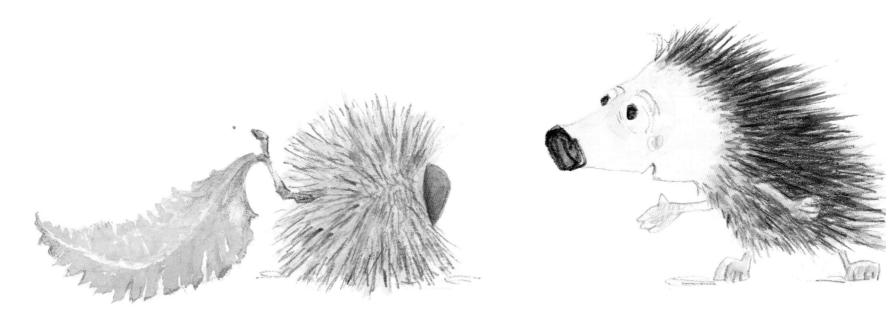

Rosie Wellesley

PAVILION

The evenings were darkening and the leaves were turning gold. It was the time when hedgehogs should be settling for their winter sleep.

But Isaac the hedgehog was NOT feeling sleepy.

Isaac wanted to play.

But who would
play with Isaac?

"Play?"
asked the
squirrels.

"What a suggestion! We are
too busy storing food for such
nonsense. Go to sleep Prickly One,
cold winter is coming."

But Isaac was NOT feeling sleepy.

"No time for play, we are off, off, off," chirped the swallows.

"We must fly south to the warm.
You go too, go to bed, Mister Isaac,
go to bed or you will catch cold in the winter."

But Isaac was not cold, and he did not want to go to bed.

Isaac wanted to play.

"Play?" yawned the dormouse,
"Of course yes, yes, certainly we must.
I'll be right with you.

"Mmmmm.
Wait one minute, just
one minute and I'll...
be...rgnughh...
...I'll be...

"Sxgnugh,
sssxxxksxugh..." and
he started to snore.

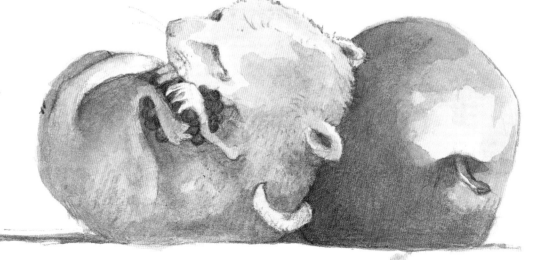

'Oh dear,' thought Isaac.
'I only want some fun.
Will nobody play with me?'

Just then he heard
a whisper close up
in his ear.

"Isssssssaaac,
I will give you one last play before winter."

Isaac jumped
up, but no one
was there.

"**Where are you?**"
He cried.

"Shhhhhhhh," went the whisper. "I am everywhere."

But though Isaac
looked he could see
no one at all.

"Where
are you?

Who
are you?

Come out
and play!"

"I am the one who makes the trees dance.
I help the ravens hover.

I rustle the grass and whip up the clouds.
And now, too, I shall play with you Isaac.
Hold up a finger,
                then you shall feel me."

"Is that you,
North Wind?"

"Yesssss!" she rustled.
"And though I am strong and you
are small we shall play together."

She held her breath.

"Are you maybe too small to play catch-a-leaf?"

Isaac was NOT too
small for this game.

Wind threw the leaves up and Isaac leapt

and he tumbled

and snatched at them falling

until he was quite pink.

But catch
them he did.

"Tut tut,"
smirked the squirrels.

"That is surely no way to behave before bedtime,"

and they scurried off out of the
breeze to their shelters.

"So," said the wind,
"it seems you are not too small for that game.
But are you too quiet for the roaring game?"

Isaac was NOT too quiet for this game.

Isaac roared at the wind, and she roared back in his ears until both their voices were spent.

Nor was Isaac too
slow for the
spin-round-and-
round game,

though Wind
tickled his nose.

"Aaa aaa atchoo!"

When at last Isaac got tired he lay on his back and looked at

the sky while Wind drew pictures for him with the clouds.

"Wind," said Isaac, "I wish I could see you,

"and I wish I could hold you, too."

Wind sighed, "But, Spiny One, some of the best things can neither be seen nor be held, yet they are real."

"Like happiness?"
yawned Isaac.

"Like happiness," smiled Wind.
"And sleepiness too.
Come little friend, cold winter is coming."

Wind ushered Isaac to his pile of leaves.

"What a nice play we had," she whispered, "but now it is time for your long winter sleep. When you wake it shall be spring and the world will be growing again."

"I'm really not sleepy," said Isaac.
"Will you sing to me, Wind?"

So Wind whistled around him
while Isaac snuggled up warm
and waited for sleep,
and for spring.